Charles Hosmer Walcott

Sir Archibald Campbell of Inverneill

Charles Hosmer Walcott

Sir Archibald Campbell of Inverneill

ISBN/EAN: 9783744761475

Printed in Europe, USA, Canada, Australia, Japan

Cover: Foto ©Raphael Reischuk / pixelio.de

More available books at **www.hansebooks.com**

Sir Archibald Campbell

OF INVERNEILL

Sometime Prisoner of War

In the Jail at Concord, Massachusetts

CHARLES H. WALCOTT

Illustrated

Printed for the Author by Thomas Todd

Beacon Press

14 Beacon Street, Boston

LIST OF ILLUSTRATIONS.

PREFACE.

THIS sketch of the life of a distinguished British officer arises indirectly from researches made at various times, for several years past, into the history of my native town. Shattuck's History does not mention Campbell, and later writers, who have alluded to his confinement in the old Concord jail, have given us no particulars as to his early life, or how he was taken prisoner, or what were the later fortunes of his life. Faint suggestions were encountered here and there of a distinguished career and a monument in Westminster Abbey, but the name Archibald Campbell was borne by many contemporaries in Scotland, and who could identify the distinguished general who reposes in the famous Abbey as one and the same with the prisoner of Concord? It was enough to excite one's curiosity to learn who our sometime prisoner really was, how he came to be a prisoner, how long he remained here, and what became of him afterwards. As the inquiry proceeded it became evident that we were dealing with no ordinary man; one question led to another, friends on both sides of the Atlantic lent kindly aid and encouragement, and now that it is finished, the author ventures to hope that this sketch will be thought to possess some interest and value as a contribution to the history of our country at a time when its great destiny depended upon the true judgment and steady purpose of George Washington more than upon all else besides.

Thanks are due to my friends, Mr. Edward W. Emerson and Miss Alicia M. Keyes, of Concord, for much valuable assistance and advice. For the beautiful photographs of Inverneill House and of the family portraits preserved there I am indebted to the kindness of Lieutenant-Colonel Duncan Campbell, the present proprietor of Inverneill House, and to Miss Jane K. McDonald, of Gareloch.

CONCORD, MASS.,
October, 1898.

SIR ARCHIBALD CAMPBELL.

Towards the last of April in the year 1776, at Greenock, on the west coast of Scotland, the 71st Regiment of Highlanders embarked for New England to assist in the work of suppressing the rebellion which had arisen in these parts.

The colonel of the regiment was Simon Fraser, Lord of Lovat and member of Parliament, by whose exertions mainly and at whose expense this force was raised expressly for service in America. Sir William Erskine, afterwards quartermaster-general at New York, was lieutenant-colonel of the 1st battalion; the senior officer of the 2d battalion was Lieutenant-Colonel Archibald Campbell, and next in command was Major Robert Menzies — all of them brave, experienced, and trustworthy officers. General David Stewart says of the officers of this regiment:

"Sir William Erskine, Sir Archibald Campbell, Major Menzies, Major Macdonell of Loch Garry, and Major Lamont were officers of great experience and approved talents, while three-fourths of the others were accomplished gentlemen."

Of these, Campbell was born August 21, 1739, at the castle of Dunderaive, near Inverary, now in ruins, where his father, James Campbell of Inverneill,[1] was then living as Chamberlain of Argyll. James Campbell was also Commissary of the Western Isles, and Hereditary Usher of the White Rod for Scotland.

In the spring of 1776 Archibald, the second son, was in his thirty-seventh year, and had already seen considerable service in the army. From 1757 to the peace of 1763 he served in the corps of engineers, most of the time as captain, and took part in an expedition to the French coast, in the conquest of Guadaloupe, Dominique, Martinico, and St. Lucia, and in the conquest of Granada. After peace was re-established the position of chief engineer in the Venetian service was offered him, with high rank and emoluments, but he preferred rather to go to Bengal in 1767 as chief engineer, with the rank of lieutenant-colonel. During the following six years, to quote the words of his younger brother, Campbell "acquired additional marks of distinction from his sovereign, and an independent fortune, with an unblemished reputation." In 1774 Lieutenant-Colonel Campbell was elected

---

[1] A view of Inverneill House is here given reproduced from a recent photograph. It is situated on the west shore of Loch Fyne and is surrounded by magnificent timber, especially silver firs of enormous size. The garden is said to be the oldest walled garden in the county of Argyll, and has curious serpentine walks, quaint circular turrets, and high stone archways.

representative in Parliament for the district of Boroughs of Stirling, etc., but, upon the outbreak of hostilities in America, he co-operated with Fraser in raising the 71st Regiment of Highlanders, which, as already stated, set sail from Greenoch in the spring of 1776.

The regiment was embarked upon seven ships and was accompanied by an armed vessel as convoy. The transports were also armed for their own defense, as will hereafter appear.

The names of the transports were the " George," " Experiment," " Annabella," " Millham," " Henry and Joseph," " Lord Howe," and " Ann," each carrying about one hundred men and officers. Campbell was on board the " George," which carried an armament of three four-pounders and two three-pounders. The sailing orders for the fleet are preserved in a book which has recently come into the possession of the Concord Antiquarian Society through the kindness of Mr. Benjamin Derby.[1] Minute

---

[1] This interesting relic was recently discovered in an attic and contains sixteen closely written pages of orders, etc., including a "quarter bill," assigning to the men on the "George" transport their respective positions in case of action, and the rolls of the first second, and third watches on the same vessel. Only a small portion of the book was actually used for the purpose for which it was intended. It became the spoil of war, and passed into the possession of Edward Heywood, a cooper, who turned the book end for end and wrote on the inside of the cover: "Edw⁴ Heywood, his Book, September y⁰ 28, 1778." The entries made by him show that it was used as an ordinary book of accounts down to 1809.

directions were herein set down for preserving the health of the soldiers. The bedding was to be brought on deck and thoroughly aired every day when the weather should permit. The berths were to be swept clean and sprinkled with vinegar, and "pitch pots" burnt between decks " to improve and correct the air." Ventilators, or windsails, were to be used to convey fresh air below the decks, ports and scuttles were required to be thrown open as often as possible, and other regulations were made for the health and comfort of the voyagers. The men were to be frequently exercised in the use of arms, especially in priming, loading, leveling and firing at a mark. They wore the Highland bonnet, red regimental coats, and vests of the same color, which, however, it may be inferred, were sometimes worn, on informal occasions, with the red side next the person. The soldiers were also supplied with "frocks;" and in case of alarm in the night time, the orders were that they should "put on their frocks or the readiest Cloathing without distinction," but if an alarm should be given by day, coats and vests must be donned, " the red sides out." Officers and men were divided into three watches of four hours each, lights and fires were required to be put out at eight o'clock in the evening, and careful provision was made for the care of the sick, as well as for guarding the powder and liquors. For

arms the men were supplied with fire-locks, swords, cartridge-boxes and shot-pouches.

In the third week of the voyage a violent gale arose and separated the fleet from the convoy, scattering the transports in all directions. Some found their way safely to New York; but the " George," " Experiment," " Annabella," " Millham," and " Henry and Joseph " remained together for some time longer, and on May 18 Campbell assumed command of the fleet, or all that remained of it, and issued new regulations prescribing signals by means of which he could communicate with the other transports, and they with him.

After seven weary weeks at sea, the " George " and " Annabella," bearing two companies of the 71st Regiment, sighted Cape Ann, and at daylight on June 16 they were at the entrance to Boston harbor.[1] No vessel had been met which could have given them any news, and they were in complete ignorance of the fact that the town had been evacuated by the British forces even before the expedition had set out

[1] Campbell says that it was "on the 17th at daylight," but apparently he is in error, for Price's diary, printed in the Proceedings of the Massachusetts Historical Society, Vol. 7, p. 257, states, under date of "Sunday, June 16," that firing was heard in the bay that afternoon, and that the prisoners were landed on the 17th. General Greene's order about the funeral was issued on the 18th, the day on which Major Menzies was buried.

from Scotland. Banks, the English commodore, was blamed for not leaving behind him one or two cruisers to warn vessels that might approach the harbor;[1] but, in point of fact, he lingered in the lower harbor with his fleet, presumably for this very purpose, as late as June 14, nearly three months after the evacuation of the town, and was at last driven away by a vigorous cannonade directed from Hull and Paddock's Island and Long Island. These timely operations of the Americans, planned by General Benjamin Lincoln, were successfully carried out under the direction of Colonel Whitcomb[2] only two days before the ill-fated transports arrived at the mouth of the harbor with the re-inforcements.

In the confident expectation of a friendly welcome, and eager to reach the land and the end of a tedious voyage, the luckless expedition, without a convoy, headed for the inner harbor. They knew not that the "Ann" transport, under command of Captain Hamilton Maxwell of the 1st battalion, had already been waylaid, a week

---

[1] Thomas Jones, in his History of New York during the Revolutionary War, Vol. 1, p. 54, complains that no cruisers were left behind by Commodore Banks to warn approaching vessels, and says that "one or two frigates stationed in the bay would have prevented all this mischief." According to Stewart, "a ship was left behind to give notice to ships not to enter the harbour, but was itself blown off in a gale of wind."

[2] Frothingham, Siege of Boston, p. 314, note; Bowen's Life of Benjamin Lincoln, p. 229.

before, by privateers who carried ship and cargo into Marblehead;[1] and even if they had known this, it is not likely that a different course would have been taken, for, according to their latest information, Boston was an English post and the place of their destination.

How the transports were attacked and how nobly they acquitted themselves is best told in the language of the lieutenant-colonel commanding, in his report to Sir William Howe dated at Boston June 19, 1776. The battle, which from a military or naval point of view was creditable to all concerned, has not received much notice from the historians, with the one exception of Dr. William Gordon, who appears to have been mainly indebted for his information to Campbell's report:

"We found ourselves," says Campbell, "opposite to the harbour's mouth of Boston, but from contrary winds it was necessary to make several Tacks to reach it. Four Schooners, which we took to be Pilots or armed vessels in the Service of His Majestie (but which was afterwards found to be four american Privateer of 8 Carriage guns, 12 Swevells & 40 men each), were bearing down upon us at 4 o'clock in the morning. At half an hour thereafter two of them engaged us and about 7 o'clock the other two were close alongside.

The George transport, on board of which Maj[r] Menzies & I with 108 of the 2[d] Batt[n] the adjutant,

---

[1] On June 10 the parole given out at the headquarters in Boston was "Highlanders," and the countersign was "Taken." Mass. Hist. Soc. Proc., 1878, p. 357.

the Q^r Master 2 Lieutenants and five Volunteers were passengers, had only six piece of Cannon to oppose and the Annabella, on board of which was Capt. M'Kinzie together with 2 Subalterns volunteers and 82 private of the 1st Batt^n, had only two Swevells for her defence — under such Circumstances I thought it expedient for the Annabella to keep ahead of the George that our artillery might be used with more Effect and less Obstruction. Two of the Privateers having stationed themselves on our larborde Quarter and two upon our Starboard quarter, a tollerable Cannonade ensued which with very few intermissions lasted till four in the Evening when the Enemy bore away and anchored in Plymouth harbour. Our Loss upon this occasion was only three men mortally wounded on board the George; one killed & one man slightly wounded on Board the Annabella.

As my orders were for the Port of Boston I thought it my Duty at this happy Crisis to push forward into the Harbour not doubting I should receive protection either from a Fort or some ship of Force stationed there for the Security of our Fleet. Towards the Close of the Evening, we perceived the 4 Schooners that were engaged with us in the morning joined by the Brig Defence of 16 Carriage Guns 20 swevells & 117 [men] and a schooner of eight Carriage Guns 12 swevells & 40 men get under way and make towards us. As we stood up for Nantasket road an American Battery opened upon us; which was the first serious proof we had that there could scarcely be any friends of ours at Boston; and we were too far Embayed to retreat especially as the wind had died away and the Tyde of flood not half expended. After each of the vessells having twice run aground we anchored at Georges Island[1] & prepared for action, but the Annabella by some misfortune got aground so far astern of the George, we could expect but a feeble

---

[1] Now occupied by Fort Warren, the principal defense of the harbor.

support from her musquetry. About 11 o Clock two of the Schooners anchored right on our Bow and one right astern of us. The armed Brig took her Station on our Starboard side at the distance of two hundred yards and hailed us to strike the British Flag. Altho the mate of our Ship, and every Sailor on board (the Capt. only excepted) refused positively to fight any longer, I have the pleasure to Inform you that there was not an officer non-commissioned officer or private man of the 71st, but stood to their Quarters with a ready and chearful Obedience. On our refusing to strike the British Flag the Action was renewed with a good dale of warmth on both sides and it was our misfortune after the sharp Combat of an hour & one half to have expended every Shot of our artillery. Under such Circumstances hemmed in as we were with 6 Privateers in the middle of an Enemy's harbour, beset with a dead Calm, without the power of Escaping or even the most distant hope of releife I thought it became my duty not to sacrifize the lives of Gallant men wantonly in the Arduous attempt of an evident impossibility. In this unfortunate affair Major Menzies & 7 private Soldiers were killed, the Q^r Master and 12 private soldiers wounded. The Major was burried in Boston with the Honours of War.

Since our Captivity I have the honour to acquent you we have experienced the utmost Civility and good treatment from the people in power at Boston, in so much Sir, that I should do injustice to the feelings of Generosity, did I not make this particular information with pleasure & Satisfaction.

I have now to request of you that so soon as the distracted state of this unfortunate Controversy will admitt you will be pleased to take an early oppertunity of settling a Cartell for myself and Officers." [1]

---

[1] In Almon's Remembrancer (Vol. 3. p. 289) is what purports to be a copy of the lieutenant-colonel's report, and I have in my pos-

The side arms of the officers were restored to them, and the Colonel was pleased to report to his superior officer the "utmost civility and good treatment" received from the people of Boston.

Ezekiel Price, a Boston man, wrote in his diary under date of "Sunday, June 16," that the firing of cannon was heard in the bay that afternoon; and on the next day he was at Boston and saw the officers land on Long Wharf and pass up King Street on their way to General Ward's headquarters. Great numbers of people were in the streets. General Greene's orderly book contains an order issued on the 18th, that "the Highland major, who was slain in the last engagement on board the ship, is to be buried this afternoon from the State House. The Scotch officers will walk as mourners, and all the officers in town off duty are desired to walk in the procession."

The commanding officer of the expedition was fully justified in saying that, everything considered, the result did not reflect dishonor upon the officers and men under his command. Great, however, must have been the exultation of the Americans, whose pluck and persistency had at

session a MS. copy sent by Campbell at the time to his kinsman, Captain Archibald Campbell, for the information of his friends at home. This copy was recently obtained through the kindly offices of Mr. Duncan Campbell of Craignish, and as it differs in some material particulars from the printed report, I have thought best to follow the manuscript.

length been rewarded by the capture of an officer of high rank, together with half his regiment, before they could strike a blow in the enterprise for which they were really enlisted. Officers and men fought bravely until their ammunition failed, but with such opponents to contend with, and under all the adverse circumstances of the case, defeat was inevitable. We note with pleasure the courtesies extended by the victors to the vanquished, and are glad to know that, thus far, at least, our rough, untutored militia had in no respect fallen short of what Campbell and his brother officers might have expected from veterans trained in all the etiquette and discipline of European armies.

On the 19th, while Campbell was writing his report, Captain Lawrence Campbell, in command of the transport "Lord Howe," stood into the harbor all ignorant of what had happened, and he too was taken into camp by the insatiate rebels.

The situation at Boston was by no means free from embarrassment; for, as a result of these operations, more than four hundred (some contemporary accounts say, seven hundred) prisoners of war were suddenly thrown into the hands of a people who had no sufficient means of properly securing and caring for their unwilling guests. There was also good reason to fear that Commodore Banks, in his slow progress towards Halifax, might touch at some intermediate point, and, learning of the captures in Boston harbor, feel impelled to take advantage of any favorable wind that might offer, and seek an opportunity of doing something to lessen the force of the adverse criticism which he was sure to encounter when news of the disaster should be received by the British commander-in-chief.

In May preceding the Continental Congress had ordered that all persons taken in arms on board any prize should be deemed prisoners of war, to be taken in charge by the supreme executive power in the colony to which they might be brought. Officers were not to be permitted to reside in or near any seaport town or public post-road, nor were officers and privates to be suffered to reside in the same place. Secure places must be found in the more remote inland towns, from which escape would be difficult, and where the chances of a successful rescue would be least. It was further ordered by Congress that officers should be allowed to give their parole, if they were willing, those who refused to be committed to prison. Prisoners who were not officers might be permitted to exercise their trades and to labor for the support of themselves and their families.

Such, in general, were the directions of the Continental Congress to the Council of Massachusetts, then the supreme executive power in the province ;

and, accordingly, on June 20, the Highland prisoners were ordered to the interior, in squads of
one hundred to each of the principal counties.
The officers were paroled ; but the sheriff desig-
nated in each order was required to deliver to
the Committees of Correspondence, Inspection,
and Safety, in the several towns, all the private
soldiers who were willing to labor under the
direction and inspection of the town committee
in the exercise of their trades, and to confine in
the county jails all who were not so inclined.

The Highlanders of the eighteenth century are
not usually associated in our minds with any occu-
pation so tame and commonplace as a useful trade ;
nevertheless, upon the rolls of this regiment men
are described not only as common laborers, but
there were also flax dressers, shoemakers, tailors,
weavers, plasterers, wrights and smiths, a salter, a
farmer, a gardener, a butcher, a land surveyor, a
stocking weaver, a baxter [baker's lad], a road-
maker, a nailer, and one merchant — making
altogether a company of varied talents and
capacity for usefulness that would have been
a valuable accession to any colony. At this
particular time, however, their purpose was the
opposite of peaceful ; they had accepted the king's
shilling, for the time being their trade was war,
and to most of them an idle life in jail seemed
preferable to working at their trades unfettered,

but under the galling espionage of a Committee
of Inspection.'   Lieutenant-Colonel Campbell and
seven other officers were ordered to the town
of Reading and found quarters in the house of
Captain Nathan Parker, which is yet standing
near the railroad station in that town, in the
West Parish, now Reading.

A retinue of twenty-two servants, including
four women and two children, went down into
the country to minister to the comforts and
pleasures of this band of eight. Among them
were a cook, a carpenter, a shoemaker, a tailor,
and a piper.   The officers were allowed to go
about freely within a radius of six miles; and,
between the cook and the piper, life was not so
dull in Reading after all. But the plain country
people, unused to such splendor of bearing and
quaintness of apparel, looked with disfavor upon
the gay, red-coated strangers whose outlandish
costume and music disturbed the customary
serenity of their village, and whose repeated
demands upon the public treasury to feed and
clothe the servants of their luxurious habits were

' In one of Campbell's letters it is stated that the soldiers were
expected to work for their captors without pay; but if this require-
ment was ever insisted upon it was soon waived, for in a letter from
Col. James Bowdoin, President of the Council, August 23, 1776, he
says, that of the Highlanders many and perhaps the largest part of
the privates were "by their own consent at labour for their subsistence."— Mass. Archives, Vol. 195, p. 447.

well calculated to offend the frugal, self-denying farmers of Middlesex, as well as the "people in power" at Boston.

Before long the supplies for the servants became irregular, and then ceased altogether, the honorable council thinking it "highly reasonable" that the officers should either support their servants, or dismiss them and allow them to go to work. Accordingly, we find, about the middle of August, that the lieutenant-colonel had dismissed four of his servants. One went to work at his trade of shoemaking; the other three, refusing to work, were lodged in jail. Campbell hired a house in Reading and continued to live there comfortably with his companions and servants, until the capture of General Charles Lee, in December, 1776.

The grief and sense of loss everywhere felt by the Americans upon hearing of the capture of Lee were succeeded by feelings of indignant resentment when it was learned that General Howe, the British commander-in-chief at New York, refused to entertain any proposition for the exchange of Lee, although Campbell and five Hessian field officers were offered as an equivalent for the dashing but erratic general. Howe's orders from the English government even required him to send Lee to England by the first ship of war, to be tried there as a deserter from the English army; but the British commander, in the exercise of a superior discretion, chose to disregard this part of his instructions, and in consequence of the representations made by him the government's mandate was withdrawn or qualified in this respect. Then it was that, through a curious combination of popular feeling and misconception of material facts, Campbell's fortunes became so closely involved with Lee's as to require much of the attention of the chief commanding officers on both sides.

The demand for retaliation upon the prisoners in the hands of our people grew out of the widespread belief that Lee was being maltreated, and this demand was stimulated by the order of the English government that Lee should be sent to England to be tried for his life before a military tribunal. The harsh treatment of Ethan Allen, lurid accounts of Indian atrocities on the frontiers, the excessive zeal of the tories, and other alleged outrages, either perpetrated or connived at by the British, were cited as just grounds for retaliation.[1] The order of Congress, passed January 6, 1777, was as follows:

Congress being informed that Major-General Lee hath, since his captivity, been committed to the custody of the provost, instead of being enlarged on his parole, according to the humane practice that has taken place

---

[1] Almon's Remembrancer, Vol. V, p. 139.

with officers of the enemy who have fallen into the hands of the American troops — a treatment totally unworthy of that gentleman's eminent qualifications, and his rank in the service of the United States, and strongly indicative of farther injuries to his person :

Resolved, That General Washington be directed to send a flag to General Howe, and inform him that, should the proffered exchange of General Lee for six Hessian field officers not be accepted, and the treatment of him as above mentioned be continued, the principles of retaliation shall occasion five of the said Hessian field officers, together with Lieutenant-Colonel Archibald Campbell, or any other officers that are or shall be in our possession equivalent in number or quality, to be detained, in order that the same treatment which General Lee shall receive may be exactly inflicted upon their persons.

Ordered, That a copy of the above resolution be transmitted to the council of Massachusetts Bay, and that they be desired to detain Lieutenant-Colonel Campbell and keep him in safe custody 'till the farther order of Congress, &c.

On February 20, the situation having apparently undergone no change, Congress further

Resolved, That the Board of War be directed immediately to order the five Hessian field officers and Lieutenant-Colonel Campbell into *safe and close custody*, it being the unalterable resolution of Congress to retaliate on them the same punishment as may be inflicted on the person of General Lee. — *Journal, February 20th, 1777.*

This order had already been anticipated by the authorities of Massachusetts, who, upon receiving notice of the preliminary resolve passed January 6 had ordered that Lieutenant-Colonel Campbell's parole be annulled, and that he be placed in the keeping of the sheriff of Middlesex; and on February 1, 1777, the prisoner was committed to close custody in the jail at Concord.

This jail, or " goal," as it is almost invariably spelt in contemporaneous writings, was a wooden building standing upon ground adjoining the West Burying-Ground, on Main Street, and now forming part of the estate of the late Reuben N. Rice. It was two stories in height, was built of logs and had a four-sided roof. Near the end of the last century it was superseded by a larger structure of stone which stood, until about thirty years ago, behind the space between the Middlesex Hotel and the County House, now occupied by the Rev. E. J. Moriarty. A picture of the old wooden jail, which is said to be a drawing made by Campbell, hangs in the Concord Public Library and shows the building as it appeared in Revolutionary times. Within the recollection of persons now living it was used as a hatter's shop, and later as an adjunct to the stable of Bigelow's Tavern, long since demolished.

The old jail was built in the year 1755, and first stood on land bought of Jonathan Heywood, and situated on Walden Street near the house now owned by Concord's Home for the Aged. It adjoined Heywood's house on the northwest side,

was thirty feet long and twenty-six feet wide,
exclusive of entry and stairway. The sides and
lower floor of the building were of timber seven
inches in thickness. The plan for its construc-
tion provided that it should be " divided into four
rooms " on each floor.

In January, 1756, it was reported ready for the
victims of the law, and Jonathan Heywood, a tan-
ner by trade, was appointed under-keeper and
soon afterwards obtained an innholder's license.
It was common in those days, here and elsewhere
— the combination of a jail with a tavern, both
under one management. It was a thrifty arrange-
ment; for imprisoned debtors could obtain the
privilege of the "liberties" of the jail by giving
a bond that they would not attempt to escape;
and the superior accommodations afforded by the
inn close by, compared with the ill-kept rooms and
wretched fare of the prison, caused many a shilling
to be diverted from the pockets of the prisoners to
the landlord's capacious purse. No one then had
any thought of prison reform in the modern sense
of the term, but in 1769 complaints from some
source were loud enough to make the Court of
General Sessions of the Peace aware of the fact
"that the Limits of the Prison Yard were very
much too contracted and thereby rendered very
nauseous & unwholesome, and also by Reason of
Gutters for the Wash and Filth of the Prison

Keeper's House &c That the Prisoners for Debt & others are debarr'd from Water unless they purchase the same." The lot on which the jail stood contained only about one-sixteenth of an acre, and, as Mr. Heywood was unwilling to part with any more land, the county bought of Captain Ephraim Jones a dwelling-house and about one-quarter of an acre of land next to the burying-ground on Main Street, and in the early spring of 1770, when there was yet a little snow on the ground to make things slip along easily, the jail was removed to the new lot, under the superintendence of Joseph Hosmer, whose courage, integrity, and sound judgment five years later, at the North Bridge, and subsequently throughout the war, won the confidence and respect of his fellow citizens. The removal was facilitated by the use of rollers, and green trunks of trees, called "shoes," which, being made fast underneath, slid over the slippery ground like the runners of a sled. Twenty-six pairs of oxen drew the load, and no doubt large and interested groups of spectators were at hand to watch the passage of the home of debtors and malefactors along the road by the mill-pond, around the corner by the old mill, and past the burying-ground to the new location prepared for it. From this time onwards it was connected with Jones's Tavern, afterwards Bigelow's, and Captain Ephraim Jones was appointed keeper under the sheriff of the county.

I find no annals of this fortress of the law before the outbreak of the Revolution. On the 20th of April, 1775, some British soldiers wounded and captured on the preceding day were confined here, and from time to time during the war tories and prisoners-of-war were consigned to its unpitying chambers, in obedience to the orders of the Council at Boston, or of a local inquisitorial board, called a committee of correspondence or committee of inspection. There are interesting memorials of persons confined here, of officers of the "Falcon" ship-of-war and the schooner "Volante;" of Dr. Josiah Jones and Dr. Jonathan Hicks, notorious and troublesome tories, who, after sending out ingenious and unavailing protests, were fortunate enough to be able to cut the knot of their difficulties by effecting their escape. There, too, was young Robert Campbell, only seventeen years of age, who was taken at Falmouth, and proudly informed the committee who were appointed to examine and search him, that he was "son of Lieutenant-Colonel Alexander Campbell, who is now Lieutenant-Governor of Fort George in Inverness, and is one of the first families in Scotland." In the language of the report, "said Robert Campbell further says he was born in ye army & now has a Recommendation for an Ensign's commission in the 35th Regiment."

On September 25, 1775, a petition was for warded by Sergeant Matthew Hayes, eight privates of seven different regiments, and one marine, representing that the signers had been confined in this jail as prisoners of war "ever since the 19th day of April last," and that they were in need of suitable clothing to cover their nakedness in the approaching cold season. They were, in fact taken on the 19th, but were not sent to Concord until the 25th, as appears by the following letter from General Ward to Colonel James Barrett:

HEAD QUARTERS, APRIL 26th, 1775.
SIR,

I am informed that there are a Number of Prisoners in Concord Goal, ten of which were conveyed thither yesterday that were taken in the late Skirmish, who have since that unhappy Event, been at Newton & done some Labour; but being absent I cannot judge so well whether it is safe to trust them as you may on the spot : — There-fore I refer it to you, to do with them, & any other Pris-oners of the like sort, as you may think best : pray keep them from any Infection that may arise from putting too many in one Room : — air them when necessary ; provide everything needful for their comfortable subsistence : — no doubt you have things convenient for them in Con cord ; & will be at some future time satisfied for your trouble.

I am sir &c

A. WARD.

Moved by the prisoners' petition, the Council empowered and directed Ephraim Wood, one of the selectmen, "to provide one Coat, one pair of Breeches, one pair of stockings, one shirt, and one pair of shoes" for such as were in need; with the assurance that the amount expended for this purpose would be refunded. Let us hope that the faintness of the assurance did not deter the selectmen from suitably providing for these men.

Lieutenant-Colonel Campbell was by far the most interesting inmate of the jail, and was for some time the prisoner of highest rank in the hands of the Americans. Four days after his confinement he addressed a forcible but manly and dignified letter to General Washington, describing his surroundings, and protesting, as one soldier to another, against such treatment. He addresses Washington in his supposed character of "dictator" as follows:

CONCORD GOAL, 4TH FEB'Y 1777.

SIR,

From the powers which I have lately understood has been reposed in y'r Excell'y as dictator, and from the character I have always entertained of y'r generosity of sentiment, I am naturally led to use the freedom of troubling you with the complaint of an officer, who suffers at this instant a treatment more notoriously dishonourable & inhuman than has ever existed in the annals of any modern war. Y'r Excell'y well knows that I was a prisoner at large upon my Parole of honour in the town of Reading since the month of June last;

during which period, I will venture to pronounce it is
even beyond the power of malevolent aspersion to charge
me justly with the most scrupulous violation.   The first
of this month I was carried & lodged in the common Goal
of Concord by an order of Congress, thro' the council of
Boston ; intimating for a reason, that a refusal of Gen'l
Howe to give up Gen'l Lee for six field officers, of whom
I was one, and the placing of that Gentleman under the
charge of the Provost at New-York were the motives of
their particular ill-treatment of me.   How far these as-
sertions may be founded on real matter of fact, & appear
to your Excell'cy consistent with Justice & the usual
practices in war, I shall not pretend to determine, but
when you are well informed of the real circumstances of
my present situation, of which I am persuaded you are
still ignorant, you will be a better judge of my usage,
& weigh as a soldier its propriety.   I am lodged in a
dungeon of about 12 or 13 feet square, doubly planked
and spiked on every side, black with the grease and litter
of successive criminals & completely hung around with
cobwebs.   Two small windows, or portholes, not glaz'd
but strongly grated w'th Iron on the inside and well
barricaded with shutters on the out, introduce a gloomy
light to the apartment.   Two doors doubly planked &
locked, shut me from the prisoners yard, and the Goaler
has rec'd express orders against my going into it, even
for the necessary calls of nature, and an hole near the
middle of these doors serves either to admit my victuals,
or gratify the gaping curiosity of spectators.   In the
corner of the room boxed up to the partition a wooden
necessary house stands uncovered, which does not seem
to have been emptied since the first hour of its being
consecrated to the natural ease of malefactors, and a
more loathsome black hole decorated with chains & Iron
rings well rivetted & clinched is granted me from my
inner chamber, from whence a notorious Felon was but
the moment before removed to make way for y'r humble

serv't, and in which his litter and his Excrement still
actually remain. This noisy malefactor occupies the
dungeon on my left, and a few Highlanders of the 71st.
Reg't. under the same restrictions and hardships with
myself, for having refused to work for the Americans
without pay, are my quieter neighbors on the right. I
am even refused from council, the attendance of a single
servant on my person, and every kind of intercourse or
correspondence denied, except what passes through the
medium of the Goaler. In short, sir, to complete the
whole, such is my situation, was a fire to take place in
any one of the chambers, (which are all wood excepting
the mere chimney stacks) the whole of its Inhabitants
must perish before the Goaler could go through the
ceremony of unlocking the doors, notwithstanding I
think him a man of humanity; because his house is so
remote from the Goal, any call or noise from within
might be difficult, especially in stormy weather to be
heard. I cannot also help representing to your Excell'y
the case of Capt. Jno. Walker, bearing his Majesty's
Commission in Col. Gorham's Corps. This Gentleman
is huddled into the same Goal & apartment with the
common men, a treatment highly inconsistent with his
rank.

Thus, sir, have I briefly laid before you without exag-
geration the real state of my treatment, and your own
feelings as an officer will suggest how far it is consistent
with the principles of Justice to suffer such dishonour to
be inflicted on a Gentleman, whose only crime is that of
being a Lieut. Col. in the service of his Brittannick
Majesty. When I was first taken prisoner into Boston,
I rec'd from those who took me and the controuling
power there, the fairest promises unasked, of my being
certain of Gentlemanly treatment. And your Excell'y
and they are no strangers to the Justice I render'd the
Americans by the most handsome representations to
Gen'l Howe & my friends in Britain by the letters

which lately passed thro' your hands.   But I am persuaded y'r Excell'y is still ignorant of the early shameful
return made me for a well meant endeaver to suppress
what but too often happens in such unhappy controversies
The chance of ill grounded misrepresentation.   Sir, the
truth is, that eight days had scarcely elapsed after my
first address to Gen'l Howe when I was actually plundered
of half my private property; the very necessary articles
of living, by the Continental Agent Capt. Bradford[1] of
Boston, who has since (as I am informed) seiz'd upon
and disposed of for the dirty consideration of Gain, the
very side arms of my officers, to whom they had been
restored by the captors after the action, & afterwards
lodged in the hands of Major Chase at Boston by order
of Gen'l Ward.

I should not have troubled your Excell'y with so
disagreeable a recital, were I not from my soul persuaded,

---

[1] Captain John Bradford was styled "Agent of the Continental
armed vessels." He wrote a letter indignantly denying the charges
laid at his door, but I have been unable to find it.

"The very necessary articles of living" are more particularly
described in a letter from Campbell to the Council, dated April 2.
1777 (Mass. Archives, Vol. 196, p. 357), as follows :

      1 Cask Westphalia Hams
      1 Do Corn Beef
      1 Do Salt Butter
      5 Do Containing 45 Dozen of Wine.
           ——
Total   8 casks.
    Also
        44 Dozn of Wine
        20 Dozn of Bottled Porter
        10 Dozn of Bottled Beer
         2 Cases of Portable Canteens
         2 Tents and marquees for a Field off" with their apparatus
             complete
         1 Do for servants
         1 new Spanish Cloak
         1 set of Breakfast China.

you equally abhor as I heartily despise a treatment so exceedingly cruel, mean & ungenerous, and I now look forward to you for redress.

I have the honour to be respectfully
Sir, Y'r Excell'cy's much
injured h'ble serv't,

ARCH'D. CAMPBELL Lt. Col.
71st. Regt.

His Excell'cy
   Gen. Washington.

Ten days later, on February 14, Campbell wrote to Sir William Howe a similar description of his circumstances, in order that his lot might be compared with the treatment of General Lee in New York. These letters were received about the same time, — one by Washington at Morristown, and the other by Howe at New York. Howe at once sent a courteous remonstrance to the American commander, asserting that Campbell had "an indubitable right" to be exchanged, and that putting him in close confinement was "contrary to the tenor of his parole, which is binding on both parties."

Throughout the colonies the people had been stirred up by stories of atrocities committed by the enemy, and their minds filled with apprehensions of new horrors to come. Negotiations for an exchange of prisoners were not favored by Congress and were easily hampered and obstructed in many ways, as was the case in the

war of the Rebellion. The excitement found a
vent in the retaliatory resolves passed by Congress. These votes undoubtedly expressed the
popular feeling of the moment; but Washington
showed himself superior to the easily aroused
indignation of a people engaged in a hand-to-
hand struggle, and the wisdom of choosing him
to the supreme command of the army has no
better proof or illustration than is afforded in
the conduct of this episode in our national
history. The severity shown to an officer of
Campbell's rank caused the General great annoy-
ance, at a time, too, when all his vigilance was
sorely needed for the direction of active operations at the seat of war. Here, however, was
a wrong, and he promptly undertook to right
it, so far as it lay in his power to do so.

The first thing was to write a letter, dated
February 28, to Colonel James Bowdoin and
the Massachusetts Council, in which he refers
to Campbell's letter, saying, " It gives me such
an account of the severity of his confinement
as is scarce ever inflicted upon the most atrocious criminals." The resolve of Congress,
passed January 6, 1777, is quoted in order to
show that the order of the Massachusetts Council was not justified "upon the most strict in-
terpretation of the resolve." The General then
expresses his wish that immediately upon the

receipt of this letter, the prisoner may be " removed from his present situation and put into a house where he may live comfortably." Apparently the order of February 20, addressed by Congress to the Board of War, had not yet been communicated to the Commander-in-Chief, for after touching upon other matters complained of, a postscript suggests that " Colonel Campbell's Confinement may be enlarged, without assigning the Reasons publicly." The next day Washington received notice of the new resolve and courteously replied to Campbell's protest in the following admirable letter (Sparks, " Writings," Vol. iv, p. 333):

MORRISTOWN, 1 MARCH, 1777.

SIR,

I last night received the favor of your letter, and am much obliged by the opinion you are pleased to entertain of me. I am not invested with the powers you suppose ; and it is as incompatible with my authority, as my inclination, to contravene any determination Congress may make. But as it does not appear to me, that your present treatment is required by any resolution of theirs, but is the result of misconception, I have written my opinion of the matter to Colonel Bowdoin, which, I imagine, will procure a mitigation of what you now suffer. I have also requested, that inquiry be made into the case of Captain Walker, and proper steps taken to remove all just cause of complaint concerning him. I shall always be happy to manifest my disinclination to any undue severities towards those whom the fortune of war may chance to throw into my hands.

I am &c.

In a letter to the President of Congress, of the same date, Washington says (Sparks, Vol. iv, p. 334):

I was this evening honored with your favor of the 23d ultimo, accompanied by sundry proceedings of Congress. Those respecting General Lee, which prescribe the treatment of Lieutenant-Colonel Campbell and the five Hessian field-officers, are the cause of this letter. Though I sincerely commiserate the misfortunes of General Lee, and feel much for his present unhappy situation, yet, with all possible deference to the opinion of Congress, I fear that these resolutions will not have the desired effect, are founded in impolicy, and will if adhered to, produce consequences of an extensive and melancholy nature. Retaliation is certainly just, and sometimes necessary, even where attended with the severest penalties; but, when the evils which may and must result from it exceed those intended to be redressed, prudence and policy require that it should be avoided. Having premised thus much, I beg leave to examine the justice and expediency of it in the instances now before us. . . . Gen'l. Lee's usage has not been so disgraceful and dishonorable as to authorize the treatment decreed to these gentlemen . . . Here retaliation seems to have been prematurely begun; or, to speak with more propriety, severities have been and are exercised towards Colonel Campbell not justified by any that General Lee has yet received . . . The mischiefs which may and must inevitably flow from the execution of the resolves appear to be endless and innumerable . . . Persuading myself that Congress will indulge the liberty I have taken upon the occasion, I have only to wish for the result of their deliberations after they have reconsidered the resolves, and to assure them that I have the honor to be &c.

Unwilling to let his appeal rest on this letter alone, Washington wrote an earnest letter the next day to Robert Morris, begging him to use his influence with Congress to annul the resolves. " Indeed, sir," he writes, " your observations on the want of many capital characters in that senate Congress are but too just." [1] He says that the resolves were " entered into without due attention to consequences," and were " fraught with every evil." After alluding to other business, he recurs to the matter which caused him the most concern, saying, " But the other matter, relative to the confinement of the officers, is what I am particularly anxious about, as I think it will involve much more than Congress have any idea of, and that they surely will repent adhering to their unalterable resolution." By another letter dated March 3d, Washington replied to Howe reciting what he had done in behalf of Colonel Campbell since he first heard of his situation on the last day of February, and adding: " I trust his situation will be made more agreeable, it being my wish that every reasonable indulgence and act of humanity should be done to those whom the fortune of war has or may put into our hands."

In spite, however, of the earnest remonstrances of Washington, it was resolved, on March 14, that he be informed that " Congress cannot agree to any alteration in the Resolve passed on the

---

[1] It was wittily said by Gouverneur Morris that this Congress had depreciated as much as the currency.

6th January 1777.—And as to the complaints
of Colo. Campbell, it was never their Intention
that he should suffer any other Hardship than
such Confinement as is necessary to his Security
for the purpose of that Resolve."

Upon receipt of Washington's letter of February 28, the Council of Massachusetts voted that,
"Whereas the Goal at Concord where Lieut.
Colo'l Campbell is now confined is represented
as a place quite different from what it was supposed to be when Colo'l Campbell was ordered
there to be retained and kept in Custody — there-
fore Francis Dana Esq.' is desired as soon as may
be to repair to Concord and examine into the state
of the said Goal and in case Colo'l Campbell can be
accommodated with a room in the Goaler's House,"
he is to be allowed the privilege of the yard, on
giving his parole. This partial relief was obtained
on March 6, and one servant, Peter Ferguson, was
permitted to attend him. Thus, after being confined for a month the prisoner was allowed a
larger liberty; he had a room in the tavern near
by, was allowed one servant, and was permitted
to move about in a certain limited space called
the "liberties of the jail."

On March 17, in a letter to the Council, he
gratefully acknowledges the mitigation of his

Afterwards Chief Justice of the Supreme Judicial Court of
Massachusetts.

treatment, but asks permission to return to his
house in Reading and reside there on parole.
"The motives," he says, "I had in view by such a
request were a peaceable retirement from the
tumultuous noise of a Publick Tavern, and a
reasonable deliverance from insult, to which I am
at present unavoidably exposed, from the lowest
class of passengers, and of which I experience
almost every day fresh and repeated instances,
more shameless than I would even choose to
express." This request was refused. Then came
a succession of letters in which Campbell acknowl-
edged that the treatment of him proceeded from
political necessity and misconception of facts, and
not from any desire to persecute him, and asked
that he might be permitted to live in a house with
his own servants. Concord people appear to have
treated him well. At least he calls Captain Jones,
the jailer, a kind-hearted man. He made the ac-
quaintance of Duncan Ingraham and his wife,
formerly Mrs. Merrick, who lived across the way,
and, incidentally, of young Tilly Merrick, whose
mother, Mrs. Ingraham, kindly took the stranger
into her house and nursed him when he was ill.[1]

On May 17, 1777, the Council administered a

[1] Twice during the war young Merrick had occasion to cross
the Atlantic as *attaché* to an embassy, and on both occasions was
captured by the British. The second time he was so fortunate as
to meet with Colonel Campbell, who greeted him cordially and
exerted himself in his behalf.

rebuke to " Mr. Nathan Stow Clerk of the Comt^{ee} of Correspondence &c at Concord " for permitting Campbell to send a letter to Cambridge by the hand of one of the prisoners :

"The Board are much dissatisfied with your conduct in permitting a Highland prisoner of war under your care at Concord to go to Cambridge, only to carry a Letter from Col. Campbell, which might easily have been sent by other conveyances.   This man went at large at Cambridge for three days together, and took a view of every thing, and conversed with every person he pleased.   The Board are of opinion that it is extremely dangerous to allow such liberties to Prisoners of War and expect that for the future the Com^{tee} will take effectual care that no prisoner of war shall be permitted to go without the limits of the Town.

By order of the Council."

On May 22, 1777, Howe again protested to Washington, " It is with concern I receive frequent accounts of the ill-treatment still exercised upon Lieutenant-Colonel Campbell, which I had reason to flatter myself you would have prevented.   He has, it is true, been taken out of a common dungeon, where he had been confined, with a degree of rigour, that the most atrocious crimes would not have justified; but he is still kept in the jailer's house, exposed to daily insult from the deluded populace.   This usage being repugnant to every sentiment of humanity, and highly unworthy the character you profess, I am compelled to repeat my complaints against it, and to claim immediate redress to this much injured gentleman." (Sparks, Vol. iv, p. 559.)

The American general complained to Congress that, notwithstanding his recommendation, Campbell's treatment continued to be such as "cannot be justified either on the principles of generosity or strict retaliation."

A letter written by General Lee "to the President of the State or Convention of Massachusetts Bay" (Mass. Archives, Vol. 197, p. 25), was received about this time and helped to clear up the questions of fact involved. The following is a copy:

"NEW YORK MAY yᵉ 7th 1777.

SIR

It is with the greatest concern (altho it is somewhat flattering to me) that I learn a misrepresentation of the treatment I receive has been the occasion of Colonel Campbel and some other Gentlemen Prisoners with you being closely confin'd and in other respects harshly dealt with. Sir William Howe as a servant of the Public thinks it is incumbent upon him to guard me securely but I give you my word and honour that from the beginning I have been treated with tenderness generosity and respect — gratitude truth and humanity impose it upon me as a duty to undeceive you on this head, and I am confident, the instant you are undeceived, that Colonel Campbel and the rest of the Gentlemen will have reason to be convinced that what they have suffered ought not be attributed to an illiberal way of thinking or want of humanity in those who have the direction of affairs in Boston, but to the privilege of self defence which frequently in times of civil contest obliges us to assume a severity repugnant to our natures, and I can venture to

say that severity and harshness is not the characteristic
of New England — In short I flatter myself and am persuaded that the moment you receive this note, Colonel
Campbel and the other Gentlemen will be put in the situation which their rank and character entitle 'em to.

I beg you will believe and assure the other Gentlemen
of the State that I remain, sir, your and their most de-
voted humble serv't

CHARLES LEE."

On the authority of Thomas Jones, a tory
justice of the Supreme Court of the Province of
New York, who published a history of his times,
we learn that Lee lived "in genteel apartments,
supplied at the expense of the nation with
all the luxuries that New York could afford,
had friends to dine with him, a good bed to sleep
upon, into which he tumbled jovially mellow
every night; for, to do him justice, he loved good
fellowship, a long set, a good dinner, and a con-
vivial glass, when he could enjoy them at any
other expense than his own." He says further:
"General Lee was confined in the Council Chamber in the City Hall, one of the genteelest public
rooms in the City, square, compact, tight and
warm. A sentry, it is true, stood at his door. His
fire-wood and candles were provided for him. He
had directions to order a dinner every day from a
public house, sufficient for six people, with what
liquor he wanted, and of what kind he pleased.
He had the privilege of asking any five friends he

thought proper to dine with him each day. This was all furnished at the expense of the nation. Hull, who kept the City Arms, in New York, waited upon him by General Howe's orders, with a bill of fare every morning, and Lee ordered his own dinner and his own liquors. It was cooked at Hull's and always upon the table at the time appointed. His servant had free access to him at all times."

Soon after the receipt of Lee's letter, Campbell was allowed to hire a house outside the jail limits, which he describes as " situated close under a high wooded bank, and surrounded with Marshes, in a manner totally excluded from the air and perfectly exposed to the sultry heats of the sun." He at length began to suffer from bilious fever, and was attended by Dr. Danforth of Boston and the surgeon's mate of his own regiment.

The following letter is preserved in the Massachusetts Archives (Vol. 197, f. 44):

"LIBERTIES OF CONCORD GOAL 11th May 1777
GENTLEMEN

After repeated testimonies exhibited in the Publick prints of Boston, with respect to Gen'l Lee being treated as a Gentleman in his confinement; I hope I may again be permitted the liberty of addressing the Candour of your Hon'ble Board, on the propriety of my removal from the common Goal of Concord; where I am sorry to observe, I experience at this late hour a degree of usage less becoming than the just principles of Retaliation require.

In my letter of the 17th of March, addressed to the Hon'ble The President of Council, I stated the extreme inconvenience and impropriety of my situation at Concord, together with the objects I had in view by the moderate request of a removal; and I would hope your Hon'ble Board on a Reconsideration of the matter, may be pleased at this juncture, to honour that request with a compliance; at least so far that I may be removed with my servants and effects to some retired habitation in the Country, and with a guard upon my person (if thought necessary) a ceremonious security better adapted to the distinction and feelings of a British Lieut. Col. against whom there is no personal charge, than that which I at present experience by being ignominiously placed under the charge of a Goal keeper. But should reasons of Policy render it expedient to remove me at a greater distance from Boston, than my former abode at Reading, I should esteem it a singular act of kindness in your Hon'ble Board, to fix my residence henceforth at Dunstable, or at Lancaster; towns, which I understand are pleasant in their situations, weell supplied in provisions, and where there are at this period tollerable accommodations to Lett.

I have here annexed for your Hon'ble Board the list of servants I wish to have along with me in my confinement; as they are all at Reading, one excepted who is here with me, named Peter Ferguson. I shall consider it as an additional obligation to receive your Order for their being sent to whatever quarter you are pleased to allot for my future residence; together with my Baggage and those articles belonging to me which are now lying at Reading.

Gen'l Heath having signified that an equal number of Americans ought to be released on their paroles, to compensate for the indulgence of granting me these servants, I sent him a letter of Certificate addressed to the British Commissary for Prisoners of War at Rhode Island, and I doubt not but a matter of such justice will be strictly agreed to by that gentleman on the certificate being presented.

> I have the honour to be with due respect
> Gentlemen
> Your most obed't Humble servt.
> ARCH'D CAMPBELL
> Lieut. Col. 71st. Regt.

List of Servants

Clerk — John Wilson — volunteer
Groom — David Johnston ⎫ Private Soldiers
Cook — Arch'd Silver ⎬
Do. Wife and 2 Children
Servants (William Boyd) ⎫ Not soldiers but as
(Peter Ferguson) ⎬
Prisoners of War Classed as such.

The Hon'ble Council of Massachusetts Bay."

Again, on May 26, 1777, the following letter was addressed to the Council:

" GENTLEMEN,

Lest it should not be consistent with your sentiments to grant me, even at this late period, the indulgence of being removed from the Liberties of a Goal; the following request will, I hope, be deemed by your Hon'ble Board not to interfere with the nature of that determination.

Within the Liberties of the Goal at Concord stands a house (which I understand is the County house) at present in the possession of Mr. Coverly, a Printer, who means in a few days to evacuate it. As this house has a Kitchen in it, and such other apartments as might for the present accommodate me and my servants in a tollerable degree

of Comfort, I beg leave to solicit your Hon'ble Board for
permission to Rent and occupy it, with my servants and
Baggage, till such time as it may be your pleasure to dis-
pose of me in a manner better suited to my circumstances,
as a Prisoner of War. By this indulgence I shall be freed
from the tumultuous noise of irregular Company and in a
great measure removed from that unavoidable interference
with Passengers and other visitors, to whose insults I am
even at this hour exposed by my residence at a Tavern
upon the Publick Road.

I shall nevertheless be within the liberties of the Goal,
and shall engage on my Parole of honour, that my servants
shall strictly conform themselves to the same limitations
and restrictions to which I am at present confined. The
honour of your approbation to this request will lay me
under a singular obligation, and convince me that although
I have the present misfortune to be under the present
unmerited confinement, from motives of political necessity,
yet the Generosity of your Hon'ble Board is disposed to
soften the rigour of that necessity by such an act of kindness as may render my confinement as comfortable as the
nature of the present circumstances will admit.

I have the honour to be with all due respect
Gentlemen,
Your most obedient and
most humble servant,

ARCH^{D} CAMPBELL

Lieut Colo'l 71st Regt.

Liberties of Concord Goal
May the 26th 1777.

The Hon'ble Council of Massachusetts Bay."

The following letter, which bears no date, was
addressed to one of his lieutenants, and is interest-

ing evidence of Campbell's relations to his subordinate officers:

"DEAR SIR,

It would have afforded me much pleasure to have had it in my power to agree to your being exchanged, did the Interest of His Majesty's service correspond with my wishes for your ease and comfort. For me to allow all the officers of the 71st to quit their men, on the present critical state of our affairs would indicate a degree of inconsistency in my conduct, different to what my friends would have expected of me ; and for that reason, I have determined that Lt. Fraser of the Light Infantry, Lieut. McLean of the Gren'ds, & Ensign Fraser of McKenzie's Company shall not be exchanged till something shall ultimately be determined upon with respect to the exchange of our Private Soldiers. Having hourly expectation of receiving our clothing for those poor fellows, it is necessary that an officer of each company shall take charge of the same and distribute them to the men. Surely you Gentlemen cannot expect that I must execute your duty in this respect ; or that the men when they are exchanged shall not have a single off'r to head or conduct them to quarters but the Lt. Colo'l.

I am sorry to hear of your misfortune in matters of intrigue. If the town is too Hot for you, let Fraser and you Petition to go to Dunstable ; where there is an excellent House, cheap living, and kindly neighbors to associate with, or to any more favourable spot in which you can live in peace and Quiet. Make my desire on this subject known to Ensign Fraser ; and acquaint him that there has not a single letter come from the Cartel that went to New York.

I have as yet had no account of your Clothes from Capt. Smith ; and I must tell you that I have reason to believe that Gentleman has too little interest at Boston to serve you (if occasion required) in the object of a Partial

Exchange. Content yourself, my friend, with the disappointment. Soldiers must expect such trifles now & then, but be assured, that such as it may appear to you at present, no detriment shall fall to your Lot, or that of any other of the Officers on account of it.

I am sincerely your friend

ARCH'D CAMPBELL,

Lieut. Colo'l 71st Regt.

P. S. Tell Duncanson that this letter is also an answer to his request."

On the back :

" Lieut. McLean

71st Regt   Upton."

On June 10, 1777, Washington wrote frankly in reply to General Howe :

"The situation of Lieutenant Colonel Campbell, as represented by you, is such as I neither wished nor approve. Upon the first intimation of his complaints, I wrote upon the subject, and hoped there would have been no further cause of uneasiness. That gentleman, I am persuaded, will do me the justice to say he has received no ill treatment at my instance. Unnecessary severity and every species of insult I despise, and, I trust, none will ever have just reason to censure me in this respect. I have written again on your remonstrance, and have no doubt such a line of conduct will be adopted as will be consistent with the dictates of humanity and agreeable to both his and your wishes."

At length, on August 19, Washington received authority from Congress to admit Campbell and the Hessian officers to their parole, and to propose to General Howe that they be exchanged for a like number of our men of equal rank. There was more vexatious delay, but Howe at last agreed to enlarge the officers in his hands on their parole.

In November Campbell was allowed to go and come anywhere within the bounds of Concord, upon giving his parole of honor that he would not pass beyond those limits nor give any information to the enemy.' Another weary winter passed under these conditions, but in the spring came at last the much-desired relief, and in May, 1778, Campbell was exchanged for Colonel Ethan Allen, at New York.

Thus ended a captivity of two years, during which time this capable and zealous officer had been afforded no opportunity to demonstrate

---

' The form of parole prescribed by the Council was as follows (Mass. Archives, Vol. 173, f. 572):

I Archibald Campbell Lt Colo. of the 71ᵘ Regt being made a prisoner of war by the Forces of the United State of America, do promise and Engage on my Word & honour & on the Faith of a Gentleman, that I will remain within the Limits & Boundaries of the Town of Concord in the County of Middlesex & will not Depart out of the same, during the present War between G. Britt and the United States, or untill the Continental Congress or the Assembly or the Council of the State of Massachusetts Bay shall order other-wise: And that I will not, directly or indirectly give any Intelligence whatsoever to the Enemies of the United States, or do or say any-thing in opposition to the measures & proceedings of any Congress or Assembly or any Officer of the United States, or of either of them, during the present Troubles, or untill I am duly Exchanged or Discharged. And I do likewise engage that Peter Ferguson my servant who is allowed to attend me, shall be under the same restrictions and Limitations with myself. Witness my hand this 14th Nov! A.D. 1777.

his ability as a military leader. But now he
was to have his revenge — the revenge of a
soldier. For he was soon placed in command
of a force of 3,500 men, including the 71st Regiment, who sailed to the southward from New
York in November of the same year, under
orders from Sir Henry Clinton, and escorted by
a squadron of ships-of-war commanded by Commodore Hyde Parker. The Highlanders were
mustered one thousand strong, and their fine
soldierly appearance was favorably remarked
upon in the publications of the time.

The object of the campaign was the sub-
jugation of the southern colonies and the protection of the Georgia loyalists. Savannah, the
first point of attack, was guarded by a small
force of Americans under General Robert Howe.
Major-General A. Prevost, then at St. Augustine,
was ordered by General Clinton to move north-
ward and assume the general direction of affairs
at Savannah. This order was dated October 20,
and received November 27, the very day on
which the expedition sailed from Sandy Hook.
Campbell arrived with the fleet off Tybee Island
on December 23. Learning upon his arrival
that the Americans were already informed of his
approach, that their batteries were out of repair,
that the Americans in the town were few in
number, but expecting re-inforcements every day,

Campbell pushed rapidly forward without waiting
for re-inforcements to come up, or for the slow
approach of his superior officer.   Captain Hyde
Parker, acting commodore in command of the
fleet, actively co-operated.   Our people were not
accustomed to such energy on the part of their
foes.   In the dashing impetuosity of the Highland leader there was no trace visible of the slow,
irresolute, halting tactics of Gage, the Howes, of
Clinton and Burgoyne.   The immediate results of
the new policy were startling.   By one prompt
movement vigorously pressed Savannah was taken ;
and our forces, largely inferior in numbers, be it
said, and unskillfully handled, everywhere melted
away before the determined purpose of a genuine
leader of men.   Bancroft says : " No victory was
ever more complete."   In ten days Georgia was
brought under the sway of the British, and the
campaign virtually ended — all before the arrival
of General Prevost at the scene of operations
some time after the middle of January.[1]

There is some reason to believe that the brilliant
and complete success achieved by his subordinate
in rank was not altogether pleasing to General
Prevost, and that their subsequent co-operation,
though outwardly beseeming their respective positions, was not agreeable to either.   Certain it is

---

[1] See Campbell's report to Lord George Germain, Almon's Remembrancer, Vol. 7, p. 235; Captain Parker's report, *id.* p. 244.

that Prevost adopted a plan of campaign against
the judgment of Campbell, and with the result
that most of the ground won by the skill and
prowess of the Highland chieftain was soon lost
to the British and never again recovered.

Campbell soon obtained leave of absence and
returned home to Scotland,' where, in June,
1779, he married Amelia, daughter of Allan
Ramsay of Kinkell, the painter, and son of the
poet of the same name. It is said that King
George was especially pleased with Campbell
because of his success in the Georgia campaign, and on December 7, 1779, appointed him
Lieutenant-Governor of Jamaica, with the rank
of Brigadier-General and Aide-de-Camp to the
King. Here on October 29, in the same year,
he made a report to the Earl of Shelburne
concerning two successful engagements with the
Spaniards, generously giving due credit to the
officers in command of the British forces on
those occasions.' In the year 1782 he became
Governor of the island, and in the following year
was commissioned as Major-General in the line.
In August, 1784, he returned home, bearing

'In Winsor's History of America (Vol. vi, p. 519 n.) it is said:
"This attack on Savannah is illustrated in the Faden Map (1780)
called 'Sketch of the Northern Frontiers of Georgia from the mouth
of the River Savannah to the town of Augusta, by Lieut. Col
Arch? Campbell.'"

'Southey's Hist. W. Indies, II, 534.

with him an elegant service of plate, presented by the assembly of that colony in recognition of his distinguished services.

On March 9, 1785, Campbell was appointed Governor of Fort St. George, at Madras, on the southeastern coast of India; and on September 3 in the same year he was created a Knight of the Bath. The patent from the Herald's Office bears date of December 22, 1785, and styles the recipient of the honor "Sir Archibald Campbell, Major General of his Majesty's Forces and Governour of Fort St. George in the East Indies." This appointment to the important and difficult post of Governor at Madras was conferred during the administration of the younger Pitt, and when at the head of the Board of Control was Henry Dundas, a good friend of Campbell. In 1786 Earl Cornwallis became Governor-General of India, and gave frequent testimony in his correspondence to the ability, efficiency, and zeal of Sir Archibald Campbell, whom he had known favorably in America, and of whom he had written, two years before, that he ought to have "a commission of General to command in chief in India."

Campbell's first important work in India was the new modeling of the forces of the East India Company at Madras, according to a plan submitted by him before leaving England. In

September, 1786, he was appointed by the King and the East India Company Commander-in-Chief of the forces on the coast of Coromandel, to succeed Lieutenant-General Sir John Dolling. Campbell was also mainly instrumental in the negotiation of the treaty of February 24, 1787, concerning the debts of the Nabob of Arcot, a settlement advantageous to all concerned, for which he took much credit to himself, saying: "The power of the purse and sword is now completely secured to the company, without lessening the consequence of the Nabob."

About this time Cornwallis wrote: "The most perfect harmony subsists here; no Governour ever was more popular than Sir A. Campbell;" and again, "I must do Sir A. Campbell the justice to say that he seconds me nobly. By his good management and economy we shall now be relieved from the heavy burden of paying the King's troops on the coast, and I have no doubt that his conduct will be as universally approved of in England as it is on this side of the Cape of Good Hope."

Notwithstanding this strong testimony to the efficiency and popularity of the Governor, clouds of criticism and disparagement were already gathering at home. The treaty was indeed formally approved as a whole by the Court of Directors of the East India Company sitting in London, but a hostile feeling on the part of some

of the directors was equally manifest, and every
opportunity was seized upon to attack him. The
favorable opinion expressed by him concerning
the Nabob was quoted against him, especially
when, a little later, "that venerable prince" was
openly accused of double dealing. Cornwallis at
Calcutta deprecated these attacks upon Campbell, and Mr. Dundas at the seat of government
did not fail to express his satisfaction with the
"very high opinion" expressed by the Governor-
General concerning Campbell's administration. "I
agree with you and him," he says, "that he is
very illiberally treated by the Court of Directors,
but he is not singular in that respect. We are
all (except your Lordship, as yet) sharers in it."

Again Cornwallis wrote: "Nothing could give
me personally greater concern, and nothing, in
my opinion, could be more fatal to the British
interest in India than his removal. He has shown
great ability, and the most perfect uprightness and
integrity, and possesses the esteem and confidence
of the civil as well as military part of the settlement." But these expostulations failed to impress
the management of the East India Company. An
administration of affairs that aimed to do justice,
to enforce economy, and thereby save money for
the crown did not especially interest the directors.
They wanted more lacs of rupees for the company, and, as for any sympathy with the natives,

it was, in their opinion, entirely out of place in the transaction of business in India.

A high-minded man like Campbell, earnestly desirous of administering his office honorably, faithfully, and with justice to all concerned, may withstand opposition of this sort for a season with comparative serenity, secure in the approval of his own conscience, but the time surely comes when he will not or cannot suffer it longer. Some time in the year 1787, with a full understanding of the influences which were working against him, and knowing that the opposition must in the end be successful, he gave notice that he should retire from his office and return to England early in 1789.

On October 12, 1787, he received a commission as Colonel of the 74th Highland Regiment of Foot, which was raised by himself, and was one of four that were especially designed for service in the East.[1] But notwithstanding the honors which were heaped upon him, it is only too evident that this faithful and high-spirited public servant realized that in India it was impossible for him to serve God and the King, and at the same time commend his administration to the managers of a trading corporation, whose anomalous relations

---

[1] Brown's History of the Highlands, &c. Edinburgh and London, 1859.

to the government caused frequent embarrassment to ministers of the best intentions. In February, 1789, Sir Archibald resigned his office and commission in the East, and sailed for home with health sadly impaired, and, although he had given the directors ample notice, before they were able to agree upon a successor in his office.[1]

In the following year he was unanimously re-elected to Parliament and took his seat for the district formerly represented by him, Sir James, his brother, having resigned in his favor. But the change from the climate of India to that of the British Isles was too much for a constitution already weakened by a four years' sojourn in the East. He caught cold on a hurried journey from Scotland, on being sent for to consult with the government concerning an armament which was being made ready by reason of a dispute with Spain concerning trade to the northwest coast of America. He felt obliged to decline the command which was offered him because of the state of his health, and although a visit to Bath was somewhat beneficial, death came upon him at his home in Upper Grosvenor Street, London, on March 31, 1791, in the fifty-second year of his age.

---

[1] For Campbell's life in India, see Correspondence of Charles, first Marquis Cornwallis; London, 1859; also Mill's History of British India; London, 1817.

The whole career of Sir Archibald Campbell, his letters, the letters of Washington, and the uniformly favorable comments of contemporaries, all go to show that he was a gentleman in a true and universal sense — courteous, high-minded, considerate of others, a faithful and efficient administrator of affairs, a brave and accomplished officer. In a letter of one of General Howe's field officers he is spoken of as "our worthy friend," whose capture "gives unexpressible concern to his friends, who you know are numerous." Dr. David Ramsay, the American historian, describes him as "a humane man and a meritorious officer," who, although "he had personally suffered from the Americans, treated all who fell into his hands with humanity, his course in this respect being in marked contrast with the conduct of his successors in command."

Having no issue, Sir Archibald bequeathed the greater part of his fortune to his two surviving brothers, Sir James Campbell and Commissary Duncan Campbell, in equal shares, but subject to the payment of some legacies, and a jointure to the widow of one thousand pounds sterling per year. To his nephew, Captain James Campbell, eldest son of Sir James, he gave all his military books, instruments, and drawings, also his arms, "knowing that he will never tarnish them." The brothers caused a monument to

be erected over the remains, in the Poets' Corner
of Westminster Abbey, upon which is inscribed
the following:

Sacred to the memory of Major General Sir Archibald Campbell, Knight of the Bath, M. P., Colonel of the
74th Highland Regiment of Foot, Hereditary Usher of
the White Rod for Scotland, late Governor of Jamaica,
Governor of Fort St. George, & Commander-in-Chief
of the Forces on the Coast of Coromandel in the East
Indies. He died equally regretted & admired for his
eminent civil & military services to his country, pos-
sessed of distinguished endowments of mind, dignified
manners, inflexible integrity, unfeigned benevolence, with
every social & amiable virtue. He departed this life
March 31st, 1791, aged 52. *Heu pietas, heu prisca fides
et bellica virtus. Quando Habitura Parem.*

Following is a copy of the inscription on the
stone in the floor over the grave:

Sir Archibald Campbell
of Inverneil.

Knight of the most honorable order of the Bath, Major
General of His Majesty's Forces, Colonel of His Majesty's
74th Highland Regiment of Foot, Hereditary Usher of
the White Rod for Scotland, late Governor of Jamaica,
afterwards Governor of Fort St. George and Commander-
in-Chief on the Coast of Coromandel in the East Indies.
He died 31st March, 1791, in the 52[d] year of his age.

Surely, at this distance in time the loyal sons
of America need not hesitate to award to the
memory of this remarkable man full measure of
respectful recognition, even though he was op-
posed in arms to our fathers in their great

struggle for full political rights. By reason of the hard fortune of war it was impossible, in the nature of the case, that he should have enjoyed his sojourn in Concord, but we of a later generation must needs regret that his enforced residence in our town was not made pleasanter, or at least less irksome to him. Possibly we may think it especially incumbent upon us, so far as it rests in our power, to see to it that he be remembered with that just appreciation of his merits which in his lifetime, because of untoward circumstances and the harshness born of warfare, was not bestowed upon him by our fathers.

www.ingramcontent.com/pod-product-compliance
Lightning Source LLC
Chambersburg PA
CBHW030024030726
47499CB00008B/3112